New Nanny

New
Nanny

Adapted by Lexi Ryals

Based on the series created by Pamela Eells O'Connell

Part One is based on the episode "New York, New Nanny," written by Pamela Eells O'Connell

Part Two is based on the episode "Make New Friends But Hide the Old," written by Sally Lapiduss & Erin Dunlap

DISNEP PRESS

New York

All rights reserved. Published by Disney Press, an imprint of Disney Book Group. No part of this book may be reproduced or transmitted in any form or by any means, electronic or mechanical, including photocopying, recording, or by any information storage and retrieval system, without written permission from the publisher. For information address Disney Press, 125 West End Avenue, New York, New York 10023.

Printed in the United States of America
First Edition
1 3 5 7 9 10 8 6 4 2
J689-1817-1-13166

Library of Congress Control Number: 2012953652
ISBN 978-1-4231-8369-3

For more Disney Press fun, visit www.disneybooks.com
Visit DisneyChannel.com

JESSIE

Part 1

Dear Diary,

New York, here I come! It has always been my dream to live in the Big Apple. The bright lights, the restaurants, the museums, the Broadway shows—they've all been calling my name for as long as I can remember. I grew up in a really small town in Texas, and New York just seemed like the most magical place on Earth—wait, that's Disney World!—okay, well, I guess it seemed like a place where dreams come true. And I've got big dreams. After all, how hard can it be to achieve your dreams in the greatest city in the world?

Jessie

Chapter 1

Jessie stared out the window of the cab at the skyscrapers, hot dog stands, and subway entrances of New York City, which all whizzed by at an alarming speed as she chatted with her cab driver. She was so excited she thought she might hurl— or maybe that was just due to the way the cab kept making sharp turns and screeching to a stop at red lights.

". . . So then, my dad, who's in the Marine Corps, practically blew his flattop when I said I was moving to New York, but he chilled when I told him I had a great job," Jessie explained. The cabbie had just asked her where she wanted to go, but somehow she'd ended up telling him her entire life story.

Hey! Jessie thought. Maybe he knows someone who's hiring. He did meet people all day every day, right?

"Do you know where I could find a great job?" Jessie asked eagerly.

But instead of answering her, the cab driver rolled his eyes and slammed shut the plastic divider that separated the front and back seats.

"All righty, someone needs some alone time," Jessie muttered, flipping her long brown hair over her shoulder and taking a sip of her coffee. Back in Texas, that sort of rejection would have hurt her feelings, but nothing could get her down today.

Suddenly the cab swerved around a corner,

nearly taking out an old lady crossing the street with her six dogs. Jessie slid down the bench seat and her coffee was knocked right out of her hand. She watched in horror as it landed in her purse.

"Oh, no!" she wailed, grabbing it. But it was too late; there was coffee everywhere. Jessie snatched up her phone, lip gloss, and map and hurried to dry them off on her T-shirt. Then she groped in her purse for her wallet. The last thing she needed right now was soggy money. But after a moment of searching, she realized that her wallet wasn't there. How could her wallet not be there? She'd just had it at the airport! How was she going to pay for her hotel? Or food? Or . . . the cab ride!

Jessie glanced up at the meter. She already owed twenty-two dollars and fifty cents. She took a deep breath and tried not to panic. She was a New Yorker now—she could totally handle this.

This must happen a lot. The cab driver would understand, right?

She knocked on the plastic divider and then pulled the little door open.

"Um, I'm having a little problem. My wallet is missing, so I don't have any money for the cab ride. I don't suppose I could pay you in lip gloss and breath mints?" Jessie asked hopefully. "They're wintergreen."

The driver turned and glared at her and then slammed on the brakes. Jessie pitched forward as the cab came to a halt, her cheek pressed against the plastic divider.

"Get out of my cab!" the driver roared at her.

"Okay, just give me a second to gather my things," Jessie said meekly, trying to wipe her cheek print from the divider.

"Now!" the driver yelled.

Before Jessie knew what was happening, he'd yanked her out of the car and left her standing on the sidewalk in front of a fancy apartment building. "Ow! That was rude!" Jessie exclaimed. The cab driver *definitely* did not understand her predicament.

Suddenly, Jessie's suitcase came flying through the air. It landed on the sidewalk next to her and popped open. Jessie's clothes were scattered everywhere. There was even a cardigan draped over a nearby fire hydrant.

"Hey!" Jessie yelled, her brown eyes wide. She was really angry now. Then she immediately ducked as the driver chucked her purse at her. It slammed into the building behind her and slid to the ground.

"Ha ha, you missed me!" Jessie taunted. But as she bent to pick up her purse, the driver threw her coffee cup at her, and it hit her right in the head. She fell to the ground and lay there groaning. A sidewalk full of people had just seen her get thrown out of a cab and knocked down by her own coffee cup. And now she was blocking the door of a seriously upscale apartment building. She'd been in New York for a grand total of twenty minutes, and she was already feeling like a total failure.

Luckily, there was nowhere to go but up.

As Jessie stood and started to gather her things, a handsome doorman about her age rushed over to help her. He was wearing a green and gold uniform that matched the awning above the fancy apartment building's door.

"Whoa, you must be a really bad tipper," the boy said. "I'm Tony."

"I'm Jessie," she replied as she shook his hand. He was kind of cute with his dark, messy hair, blue eyes, and soft tan.

A pretty little girl wearing a pink skirt and a sparkly T-shirt walked out the door of the building. She picked up one of Jessie's bras from the ground and brought it over to Jessie and Tony.

"I'm guessing this is yours?" the girl asked, handing the bra to Jessie.

"Yes, thank you," Jessie said, blushing. "That's just my . . . um . . . slingshot." She wasn't about to tell an innocent little girl what it really was.

"She doesn't know it's a bra," the girl said to Tony, giggling.

Jessie turned red and muttered, "Well, aren't you precocious!"

"Jessie, this is Zuri Ross. She lives in the building," Tony said.

Jessie bent down to shake the girl's hand. "Nice to meet you, Zuri."

Just then, a frazzled-looking woman carrying a

suitcase came out of the building screaming and ran down the street.

"Bye, Nanny . . . whatever your name was!" Zuri said cheerfully, waving at the screaming woman's back.

Tony shook his head and turned to Zuri. "Looks like you need a new nanny. Again."

"That was your nanny?" Jessie asked.

"Yep. She was cuckoo-cuckoo," Zuri nodded. "Hey, Jessie, you want the gig?"

"Thank you, but I didn't come all the way from Twitty, Texas, to be a babysitter," Jessie explained. She shoved her stuff back into her suitcase and zipped it closed. "I came to New York to follow my dreams, 'cause this is where dreams come true!"

"Riiight," Zuri replied, dragging Jessie into the lobby behind her. "Until then, I like my grilled cheese cut in triangles and my tutus starched."

Dear Diary,

Okay, that was embarrassing. ~~How~~ can I be a grown-up New Yorker if I can't even hold on to my wallet for five minutes? Sheesh! And this little girl thinks I'm responsible enough to be a nanny? But hey—I do need a job. It couldn't hurt to find out a little bit more, right?

Jessie

Chapter 2

Zuri pulled Jessie straight into the elevator. Jessie barely managed to pull her suitcase inside before the doors closed on it. Zuri pressed a button marked *P*, and the elevator zoomed up to the penthouse of the high-rise.

When the doors swung open, Jessie's mouth dropped open in awe. Zuri's penthouse was the coolest thing she'd ever seen. It was huge, with marble floors, sweeping views of Central Park, and an elegant staircase leading up to a second story—and that was just the living room!

"OMG! And I thought Texas was big!" Jessie exclaimed. "This is huge! And beautiful."

Zuri let go of Jessie's hand and ran over to a portly man in a stuffy suit. He was dusting a vase on a pedestal. "Look, Bertram! I found a new nanny in the street. Can we keep her?" Zuri asked pleadingly.

"If she doesn't poop on the floor, it's fine with me," Bertram answered in a monotone voice.

"Wait, don't you want to ask me any questions?" Jessie asked.

"Do you poop on the floor?" he asked Jessie in the same monotone voice.

"No," Jessie said. "Of course not."

"Congratulations. You've made the first cut. Wait here, and the parents will be home soon to interview you," Bertram said.

"Wait, you aren't the parent?" Jessie asked.

"No. I'm Bertram, the formal butler," he responded.

"You have a formal butler?" Jessie asked Zuri in disbelief. "Your life is awesome!"

Zuri just nodded. "Duh. As the nanny, you'll live here with us, you know."

"All this, and all I have to do is take care of one cute little girl!" Jessie said happily, sitting down on a plush sofa and putting her feet up on the marble coffee table. It was a pretty sweet deal—an awesome penthouse apartment to live in plus a paycheck, and she could always work on finding her dream job in her spare time.

But her relaxation was short-lived. Almost as soon as she sat down, three other children ran into the living room, yelling and chasing one another. The oldest was a pretty blond girl with big blue eyes and a seriously chic outfit. She was chasing a dark-haired boy with freckles and big brown eyes who was holding a gray ball. A shorter boy was following them, egging them on.

"Luke, give me my moon!" the girl shouted at the dark-haired boy. "I need it for my solar system!"

"I'll show you a moon, Emma!" Luke shouted back and then turned and began to pull down his pants to show her his boxer-clad behind.

"Try it, and I'll kick it into orbit!" Emma screamed. Then she grabbed a throw pillow from a nearby chair and hit him with it, knocking him to the ground.

Luke grabbed another pillow and fought back. Pretty soon, down feathers from the pillows were flying around the room as the two tried to knock each other silly.

Jessie turned to Zuri with a frightened look

on her face. "Please tell me those kids are in the wrong apartment," she begged.

"Those are my brothers and sister," Zuri replied.

"Or, as I call them, the nanny killers," Bertram added.

The shorter boy suddenly stepped forward and pushed his way between Emma and Luke. "Luke, Emma, please! Violence is never the solution," he said calmly.

"Shut up, Ravi!" Emma and Luke yelled in unison and started hitting Ravi with the pillows.

Ravi tried to protect his face with his hands, but finally he grabbed a pillow and started yelling, "To heck with the nonviolence! I am on you like stripes on a tiger!"

Jessie looked at the yelling kids and flying pillows in disbelief. How was she supposed to handle all of these kids? Zuri tugged on Jessie's shirt, pulling her attention away from the others.

"I'm the good child. Make me brownies," Zuri demanded.

Jessie sighed, rolled up her sleeves, and stepped in to break up the fight. If she let them kill one another, she definitely wouldn't get the job. She picked Luke up by his belt, but he wouldn't let go of his death grip on Emma. "Release! *Release!*" Jessie shouted, but it didn't make any difference. The kids ignored her and continued to hit one another with the pillows. "Huh, that always works with the dogs back home," Jessie muttered.

That got Luke's attention. He looked up at Jessie and stepped away from the fight, looking her up and down with admiration.

"Hello, I'm Luke. And you are?" he asked flirtatiously.

"Way too old for you," Jessie replied. "Do you guys fight like this in front of your parents?"

Before anyone could answer her, the elevator dinged and its doors opened. The kids' parents were standing inside. Their mom was a beautiful, tall blond, and their dad had wavy dark hair.

"Sometimes, but they never seem to notice," Zuri said.

The kids gave their parents another second before they all ran cheering toward the elevator for kisses and hugs. Jessie realized that she recognized them.

"Your parents are Morgan and Christina Ross? The famous movie director and supermodel-turned-business-mogul?" Jessie asked of no one in particular. She was beyond excited.

"No, they're sheep farmers," Bertram sneered sarcastically.

"Hey, guys. We missed you so much!" Christina said, scooping Zuri up with one arm and hugging Luke with the other.

"We brought presents!" Morgan added after hugging Emma and Ravi.

The kids whooped and hollered as they followed their dad into the living room to claim their presents. Caught up in the excitement, Jessie clapped and started to follow them, too. Bertram put his hand on her shoulder and pulled her back. "Not for you. This isn't *Oprah*," he said quietly.

"Dad, this is Jessie. I want her to be our new nanny," Zuri said matter-of-factly.

"So do I," Luke added eagerly.

"Nanny Kay quit? Did she say anything before she left?" Christina asked with concern.

"She said you'd be hearing from her lawyers," Emma answered.

"And then she said, 'Aaaaahhh!'" Zuri screamed.

"Hiring the nannies is Mommy's job," Morgan said, giving his wife a significant look. He turned to the kids. "Now, who wants to play with the cool toy George Lucas gave me?"

"Me! Me! Me!" the kids yelled.

Morgan pulled a Lightsaber out of his bag and flicked the power on. A jet of purple light popped out of the handle, and a low hum filled the room. It looked just like the ones in the movies.

"Whoa! Is that a real Lightsaber?" Jessie asked.

"Of course not," Morgan laughed. "It's just a prop." He swung the Lightsaber through the air like a Jedi knight. But as the purple light hit a chair, it cut the chair in half with one clean slice.

"Awesome!" Morgan exclaimed. Then his brow creased with concern. "Maybe we should go let that Ewok out of the toy chest."

He picked up Zuri and Ravi, flipped them both upside down, and ran off toward the playroom with Luke chasing him.

As the sound of giggles and shrieks faded, Christina sat down on the sofa between Jessie and Emma and turned to her daughter. "So, Emma, how's your science-fair project going? No matter what the judges said last year, I loved your glitter volcano."

"Mount Fabulous? Thanks, Mom, but this year's gonna be even better," Emma explained. "I got a clipboard and everything. I'm gonna be super science-y." She held up a hot-pink glitter clipboard decorated with feathers and rhine-stones.

Christina nodded and said, "Well, Daddy and I have to fly to the set of *Galactopus Two*—"

"Ooh, I loved the original *Galactopus*," Jessie

interrupted. "It's the best giant radioactive space octopus movie of all time."

"The critics gave it eight tentacles up!" Emma added.

"Well, we'll be back for the science fair," Christina said. "And afterward, we'll get you 'yay' ice cream, or 'awww' ice cream."

"What's the difference?" Jessie asked.

"Sprinkles!" Emma and Christina exclaimed together, and Christina wrapped her daughter in an encouraging hug.

After the kids were settled and working on their homework, Christina sat down with Jessie to discuss the nanny position over steaming mugs of tea.

Christina had her smartphone out and was scrolling through the background check she'd pulled up on Jessie while they chatted. "Okay, according to our security team, you're a straight-A student, a universal blood donor—which could come in handy with our kids—and your record is squeaky clean," Christina said warmly. Then her eyebrows arched as she read something unexpected. "Uh! Except once in third grade, you went to the bathroom without a hall pass."

"If you tasted that cafeteria food, you'd under-stand," Jessie explained, laughing. "Armadillo does *not* go down easy. And your security team is scary good."

Christina leaned forward and locked eyes with Jessie. She was uncomfortably close, and Jessie really hoped that her breath didn't smell too bad.

"Ummm . . . whatcha doin'?" Jessie asked nervously.

"Getting a read on you," Christina replied, as if her stare were completely normal. "I've made a fortune by trusting my instincts—and slapping my name on everything from sunglasses to cat food. You're hired."

"Really?" Jessie squealed. "Thank you! I promise I won't let you down." She jumped up and hugged Christina.

Luke walked into the kitchen and pulled a few cookies from the cookie jar. "Mom, can I date the new nanny?" he asked.

"The same rule applies to you that applies to Daddy. So no," Christina answered, ruffling his hair. "I'm going to go let Morgan know. Jessie, feel free to unpack and get settled."

As Christina walked out, Luke walked over and hugged Jessie. "I'm so glad you're staying," he said, and then began to slide one of his hands down Jessie's back. "Ours will be a forbidden love."

"If that hand moves one inch lower, you're gonna pull back a stump," Jessie snapped at him.

Luke's hand immediately froze on her lower back.

"Did you hear me?" Jessie asked sternly.

"Yeah. I'm just weighing my options," he admitted sheepishly.

Dear Diary,

Well, I got an awesome job and an awesome place to live, and it's only my first day here! I am killing it in New York! Of course, I still have to figure out how to take care of four kids who never seem to stop fighting. Maybe they just haven't spent enough quality time together—I can fix that. And if some togetherness doesn't work, I can always try some of the tricks I used when I trained my dogs. It's four kids; how bad can they be?

Jessie

Chapter 3

Jessie spent the afternoon getting settled in her new room. It had a king-size bed, a flat-screen TV, and a huge walk-in closet the size of her bedroom back home in Texas. It was awesome. She was seeing how many cartwheels she could complete inside of the closet (four) when a knock on the door interrupted her.

She opened it to find Luke standing outside. He was dressed in an expensive-looking tuxedo and was holding a huge bouquet of peonies.

"Hey, babe. Ready for our date?" he asked.

"We don't have a date," Jessie answered.

"But I carefully instructed Bertram to make us boeuf Bourguignonne," Luke pleaded. "With extra boeuf!"

Jessie rolled her eyes. "Hold your boeuf!"

Just then, Emma walked by on the way to her room, holding a sandwich and texting on her hot-pink phone.

"From now on, we're all going to have dinner together. As a family," Jessie announced as she plucked Emma's phone right out of her hand.

"Ew! No!" Emma squealed. "I can't eat and look at Luke at the same time."

"And don't you think having a bunch of kids on our date is kinda going to kill the mood?" Luke whined.

Jessie ignored both of them and strode over to

Zuri's door. She knocked politely and said, "Zuri? It's time for dinner."

Zuri opened the door partway and poked her head out. "I'm already eating dinner with my friend Millie the Mermaid," she informed them.

"Zuri has imaginary friends," Emma whispered to Jessie.

"I like my friends real—especially my *lady* friends," Luke cut in, wiggling his eyebrows suggestively and stepping closer to his new nanny. Jessie put one finger on Luke's forehead and pushed him back several steps. Then she turned to Zuri.

"Well, if Millie can flop downstairs, she's welcome to come eat with us," Jessie said.

"Thank you," Zuri answered. "But she won't do that. Luke makes her uncomfortable." She turned back into her room. "Have a nice dinner,

Millie." Then she shut the door and took Jessie's hand.

Jessie herded the kids over to Ravi's door. She knocked loudly. "Ravi! Time for dinner!" she hollered. There was no answer. Jessie reached out to open the door, but Luke grabbed her arm and pulled it back.

"I wouldn't go in there if I were you," he warned her.

"Why?" Jessie scoffed. "Is there an imaginary monster behind the door?" Then she opened the door.

Standing just inside was the biggest lizard Jessie had ever seen—and she'd gone to the Texas Zoo, which had some of the biggest lizards in the country. It had scaly brown and green skin, and it was gigantic. The lizard's eyes met Jessie's, and it hissed menacingly.

"Ahhhhhhhhh!" Jessie screamed and slammed the door shut. She was shaking all over. This job was getting harder by the second.

"That's Mr. Kipling," Emma explained.

Luke nodded and added, "Yeah, Ravi's giant, razor-toothed lizard."

"But I'm not allowed to have a pony?" Zuri whined. "That's cold."

Even after Jessie got the kids downstairs, things didn't go quite as she had planned. Everyone was mad at Jessie and annoyed that they were being forced to spend time together.

After a few bites, Ravi's anger got the better of him. "I cannot believe you excluded Mr. Kipling from our family dinner," he said bitterly as he looked at Jessie.

"Yeah," Luke agreed. "Mr. Kipling is the

only thing Ravi brought from India when we adopted him last month."

"I couldn't board the plane with four ounces of shampoo, and he gets to carry on a velociraptor?" Jessie muttered under her breath. These kids had no clue how lucky they were, she thought. "So, isn't this nice?" Jessie continued loudly, trying to sound more cheerful than she felt. "Would anyone like to share about their day?"

But nothing answered her except for the sound of silverware on china as the kids pushed around the food on their plates.

"I guess that's a no," Emma finally said. "Now can I go upstairs to finish my science project?" She stood up and was almost out of the door before Jessie even answered.

Jessie sighed. "Okay, okay. Fine." Convincing

these kids to get along was going to be harder than she thought.

"I must leave, too. When Mr. Kipling is alone, he gets scared," Ravi said, folding his napkin and placing it neatly on his chair.

"Of what?" Jessie asked squeakily. She couldn't think of anything scarier than that lizard.

As Ravi headed upstairs, Luke stood up. "I'm out, too," he said, narrowing his eyes. "This date was a total waste of clean underwear."

"Ew! TMI!" Jessie replied. "Go do your home-work."

"Hey! You're not the boss of me. You can't tell me what to do," he said, glaring at her.

"Actually, I kind of am. I'm your nanny, remember?" Jessie replied.

"Ooh, someone's about to flip a table," Zuri murmured gleefully.

"Well, you know what, babe? That doesn't work for me. In fact, that's it. This relationship is over!" Luke shouted. He started to stomp out of the dining room, then stopped and spun back around to face Jessie. "And to think, you coulda had all 'this.'" He flexed his muscles, did a spin, and marched out of the room.

Jessie shook her head sadly. "He is delusional," she told Zuri, her mind clearly focused on what to do about Luke. "But hey, look who I'm talking to—a girl who thinks mermaids are real." As soon as she said it Jessie realized how hurtful that would be to Zuri. "No, no, no! I meant—"

Zuri's eyes filled with tears, and she stood up, interrupting Jessie. "Millie the Mermaid *is* real!" she shouted as she ran from the room. "This is the last time I pick a nanny up out of the gutter!"

Jessie put her head down on the dining-room

table. The kids had finally agreed on something—too bad that something was hating her.

"Whoa! That was harsh," a strange voice said, booming through the dining room.

"Tony? The doorman?" Jessie asked, looking around in confusion. "Where are you?"

"I'm in the lobby," Tony answered. "Door manning."

Jessie spotted an intercom by the door and walked over to it. "And you're listening over the intercom? Spying on me?" she asked.

There was a long pause before Tony answered quietly, "No."

Then the intercom went dead, leaving Jessie all alone.

Dear Diary,

I need to do some serious damage control if I want to keep this job. The kids all hate me—and I've only been their nanny for six hours! That has to be some kind of nanny world record. ~~Hopefully~~ I can get them to forgive me before Morgan and Christina come home to fire me.

Time to break out my nana's top-secret insanely delicious chocolate chip cookies. If those don't get the kids to forgive me, nothing will. Well, the cookies plus my heartfelt apologies, of course. Wish me luck!

Jessie

Chapter 4

So far, Jessie's cookies seemed to be smoothing things over with the other kids, so she decided to try to talk to Emma next. Armed with a platter of cookies and a glass of milk, she went into the living room, where Emma was working on her science project.

Emma was making an elaborate model of the solar system. The planets even rotated around the sun, thanks to a small motor. She had her glittery clipboard out and was busy gluing planets in place when she noticed Jessie.

"Emma, is there anything I can do for you?" Jessie asked tentatively.

"You could pack your bags," Emma replied, pointing to Earth on her model. "And then go to this planet."

"That's Earth," Jessie said gently. "I'm already here."

"Oh," Emma said and pointed to Saturn instead. "I meant this planet."

Before Jessie could reply, Emma's laptop rang as a videochat call came in.

"Ooh! It's Mom and Dad!" Emma exclaimed. She pressed a few buttons, and Christina and Morgan appeared on the screen.

"Hey, honey," Morgan said.

"Hi, sweetie," Christina added.

"Don't look at my project!" Emma said, turning the laptop to ensure it wasn't pointed at her model. "I want it to be a total surprise for tomorrow!"

There was an awkward pause before Morgan said, "Em, about your project. We're really sorry, but we're not going to be able to make it."

Emma laughed. "Of course not; that would be cheating! *I'm* making it."

"I mean, my movie is way behind schedule, and Galactopus hasn't devoured Angelina Jolie yet," Morgan continued.

"And tomorrow is the only time Angelina is available to discuss endorsing my new clothing line," Christina added.

"So . . . you're really not gonna make my science fair?" Emma asked, looking crushed.

"We're really sorry, sweetie," Christina said.

"If I get too far behind schedule, the studio will fire me," Morgan explained.

"It's okay. It's no big deal. Bye." Emma flashed them a cheerful fake smile, logged off of the call, and shut her laptop.

"Emma, are you okay?" Jessie asked softly.

Emma shrugged, trying not to look too upset. "I'm used to it. They missed my tenth birthday because of the first *Galactopus*. And they'll probably miss my wedding because of *Galactopus Three*," she said, her voice rising. "Memo to Angelina Jolie: Kill that stupid space squid!"

Tears filled Emma's eyes as she ran up the stairs, nearly knocking Zuri over as she walked into the living room.

"Emma! Wait! I'll help you finish your project!" Jessie yelled. She grabbed Emma's project and ran after her—but tripped over the ottoman and landed hard on the floor, crushing Emma's solar system model.

"Ow! Oh, no!" Jessie wailed. "She'll never forgive me now."

"Don't worry, Jessie, just do what I do. Blame it on Luke," Zuri said. Then she turned and yelled up the stairs, "Luke! You're in trouble!"

The next morning, Jessie followed the kids down in the elevator, making sure everyone had their homework, lunches, and gym clothes before they went to school.

When they arrived in the lobby, Tony was holding the door open for Mrs. Bieberman, a little old lady who moved slower than molasses in January.

"Take your time, Mrs. Bieberman. And hold on to your wig. I don't want to have to chase it down in between traffic again," Tony said patiently.

Jessie stopped the kids before they got to the

door. "Good luck at the science fair, Emma. Remember, Pluto might need a little extra glue."

"It doesn't matter," Emma replied sullenly. "But thanks for staying up all night to fix what Luke broke."

"You're welcome," Jessie said guiltily.

"There's the bus!" Zuri exclaimed, pointing out the door.

The kids made a mad dash for the door, sprinting around Mrs. Bieberman and nearly knocking her over.

"Wait! Your lunches!" Jessie yelled. She hurled the lunches over Mrs. Bieberman's head for the kids to catch. Her aim was a little off.

"Ow!" Zuri yelped.

"Ouch!" Ravi whined.

"Jessie!" Luke exclaimed.

"Sorry, kids!" Jessie said, wincing as the

lunches hit the kids in their heads. "Coulda been worse! That tuna coulda been canned! Good luck, Emma."

"Enjoy your jog, Mrs. B.," Tony said as he closed the door behind Mrs. Bieberman. Then he turned to Jessie. "She only goes to the end of the awning and back. So, poor Emma's really disappointed, huh?"

"Yeah," Jessie said sadly. "I've been trying to reach her parents all morning, but all I get is voice mail. I've got to get up there fast so I can talk to them."

"Too bad you can't fly Morgan and Christina's helicopter," Tony said with a laugh.

Jessie stopped in her tracks. "But I can!" she exclaimed. "Wait, they have a helicopter?"

"Of course. Can you really fly it?" Tony asked.

"My dad taught me," Jessie yelled as she

sprinted for the elevator. "He also taught me how to survive in the desert for a month with just a compass and a toothpick. You've got the keys, right?"

"Really? Jeez, my dad didn't even play stickball with me," Tony mumbled as he grabbed the keys to the helicopter and tossed them to her.

Dear Diary,

These kids aren't so bad once you get to know them. They're actually kind of sweet. I'd be pretty cranky all the time too if my parents had missed all of my big moments. I know Morgan and Christina love their kids. They probably just don't realize how much they're needed at home. Whoops, gotta go. I'm nearing an airport and I'll need to steer this helicopter with both hands to land it!

Jessie

Chapter 5

Jessie rushed through the movie studio's soundstage. There were people everywhere, and she had no idea where Christina and Morgan might be. She was just about to try another stage when a girl wearing a headset and carrying a clipboard stopped her.

"Hey! This is a closed set," the girl said.

"I need to speak with Morgan or Christina Ross. A little girl's happiness is at stake!" Jessie replied.

The girl looked Jessie up and down and

scoffed. "You're not that little. And it's creepy to refer to yourself in the third person. This is their set, but only cast and crew are allowed in." Then she grabbed Jessie's arm and marched her out of the stage, leaving her in a hallway next to a rack of costumes.

"Ow," Jessie said, rubbing her arm. She had to get into that soundstage. She looked at the rack of costumes and had a brilliant idea. If she were dressed like a cast member, that girl would have to let her onto the set. Jessie shimmied into a space suit, pulled on boots, and snuck past the clipboard girl and onto the set.

The set was really cool. It looked like a giant spaceship, complete with shiny walls and colored lights.

"Extras! Get over here and act dead!" the clipboard girl yelled. "And remember, corpses don't chew the scenery!" She grabbed Jessie and herded her onto the set with some extras.

Jessie didn't want them to kick her out again, so she lay down on the floor with everyone else. As she put her face on the ground, Morgan walked in and sat down next to the cameraman. An assistant stepped onto the stage with a black-and-white marker and clapped it. "*Galactopus Two: This Time, It's Personal*, scene thirty-six, take one."

Christina followed, holding a thick file folder, and sat down next to Morgan. "Morgan, where's Angelina? I want her to see my designs."

"She's still in makeup," Morgan said, checking his watch. "It takes a while to apply tentacle mucus."

Jessie spotted Christina and Morgan. She stood up, all ready to deliver the speech she'd practiced the entire helicopter ride over.

"And . . . action!" Morgan yelled.

A giant black tentacle shot down from the ceiling and wrapped around Jessie's waist, lifting her into the air before she could say anything to Morgan and Christina.

"Ahhhh! Help!" Jessie screamed. She wiggled and punched, trying to free herself, but the tentacle was really strong.

"Wow, that extra's truly fantastic," Morgan whispered to his wife.

"I know. She really looks scared," Christina agreed.

The tentacle jerked around, knocking Jessie against the set walls.

"Keep your tentacles to yourself, Galactopus!" Jessie yelled. She grabbed the tentacle and yanked, pulling it from the ceiling and throwing it to the ground. "Hoo-ah!"

"Cut!" Morgan yelled. He pouted, whining, "That extra broke my tentacle!"

Jessie ran to the director. "Morgan! Christina! It's me, Jessie!"

"Jessie?!" Christina said in disbelief.

"What exactly are you doing here?" Morgan demanded.

Jessie took a deep breath and launched into her speech. "I came to tell you how much Emma wants you to be at her science fair!"

"But she said it was no big deal," Morgan said.

"She lied!" Jessie insisted.

"Oh," Christina replied. "Well, we'll make it up to her."

"When?" Jessie asked. "Look, haven't you guys ever wondered why you have revolving nannies? Your kids drive them away because they want your attention! They miss you, and even if you fire me for saying this and I lose the best job I've ever had, you guys need to start being there for them!"

Morgan and Christina looked at each other, and then turned to Jessie in unison. "You're fired," they said matter-of-factly.

"What? Wait. No!" Jessie wailed. "This is the part where you thank me for being honest with you and for caring more about your kids than I do about my job, resulting in warm hugs all around!"

"That only happens in the movies," Clipboard Girl said to Jessie as she dragged her off of the stage and out of the studio.

Dear Diary,

Well, I tried. And I failed—big time. Morgan and Christina might not have believed me that Emma really needed them to be there for her, but I know she needs someone. I'm not going to let her down. I'm flying this helicopter straight to her school to watch her present her project. Then I can say good-bye to the kids and pack up my things. After yesterday, I never thought I'd say this—but I'm really going to miss those little stinkers.

Jessie

Chapter 6

Jessie snuck into the science fair at three o'clock and sat down next to Emma and Luke in the audience.

"Did I make it in time?" she whispered.

"I'm next, but I don't care," Emma said glumly.

"Me neither. Let's bounce," Luke suggested. He stood up and grabbed his bag, but Jessie pulled him back down into his seat.

"You're staying," she said. "And you *should* care, Emma! You worked really hard on this, and you should be proud of yourself."

"But—" Emma protested.

"Emma, listen . . ." Jessie interrupted. "Just because your parents can't be here physically, doesn't mean they're not with you. They are, believe me." Jessie pointed at Emma's model of the solar system. "It's like these planets. They're far away from each other, but there's a gravitational pull that always keeps them together, right? That's what love's like. It stretches over any distance, and it's too strong to be broken."

Before Emma could respond, the head judge tapped the microphone to announce the next student. "Our last contestant is Emma Ross."

"Now you go on up there and kick some asteroid!" Jessie said cheerfully.

Emma smiled, tossed her hair back, and took her project up to the stage. As she did, Christina and Morgan walked in and stood in the back.

Emma spotted them, but Jessie didn't. Emma's frown disappeared and she broke into a huge smile.

Emma turned on her project so that all of the planets revolved around the sun. She read from her notes on her bejeweled clipboard. "This is a model of our solar system. It demonstrates that, even against massive opposing forces, one stronger force can keep everything together. That force is gravy."

The crowded giggled and Jessie cleared her throat loudly. Emma looked down at her notes. "I meant, that force is gravity," she corrected herself.

Emma curtsied and waved as the judges conferred.

"Also known as Jessie," Morgan whispered, tapping Jessie on the shoulder. Jessie turned to see Morgan and Christina behind her.

"You came!" she exclaimed. "Just like in the movies. So does this mean I'm not fired?"

Christina reached out and hugged Jessie. "You are definitely not fired."

Just then, the head judge walked back over to the microphone. "Well, students, you're all a disgrace and the reason this country is twenty-eighth in the world in science. That is, except for Preston and Emma. Great job, guys! And the winner is . . ."

Emma and Preston stared each other down across the stage. Just then, Pluto came unglued from Emma's model and fell to the ground, smashing into pieces. The audience gasped. The judge stopped mid-sentence and went back over to discuss further with the other judges. It looked like Emma's chances at winning had been shattered along with Pluto.

Jessie shook her head and mouthed to Emma, "I'm sorry. It's my fault."

"It's okay," Emma mouthed back.

The head judge came back to the microphone and announced, "And the winner, for her brilliant demonstration that Pluto is no longer considered a planet, thus smashing previous scientific theory, is Emma Ross!"

The audience broke into applause. Morgan, Christina, Jessie, and Luke all ran up onto the stage and pulled Emma into a huge group hug.

"Emma, we are so proud of you!" Christina exclaimed.

"Thank you! But why did you guys change your mind about coming?" Emma asked.

Morgan and Christina exchanged an awkward look, but Jessie jumped in before they could say anything. "Because they love you."

"And we realized being here for you is more important than any job," Christina said, giving Jessie a grateful look.

"Even if I never work for that studio again. Or any other studio," Morgan added nervously. He looked up and whispered, "Please, Lord, don't let me end up in TV."

"Let's go celebrate over a nice family dinner!" Jessie suggested.

"Dibs on sitting next to Jessie," Luke said. He put his arm around Jessie as they all walked toward the door, letting his hand slip a little ways down her back. Without even looking, Jessie pushed his hand away.

"Forget it, Freckles."

"I love victory sprinkles!" Emma exclaimed as she took a bite of her ice cream cone. The whole family, including Mr. Kipling, was enjoying ice cream in the penthouse kitchen.

Zuri was eating her ice cream from a bowl with no spoon, and her face was entirely covered in strawberry ice cream.

"Uh-oh!" she moaned. "Face freeze!"

Morgan lifted his face out of his bowl with even more ice cream smeared on his face. "Me too!" he said. "Don't you hate that?"

"Hey, Ravi," Luke asked, "what's your favorite ice cream flavor?"

"All of them," Ravi answered. "In India, we just had one kind: melted."

Everyone giggled. "I'm just so glad the whole family is together," Christina said, putting her arm around Emma and giving her a hug.

Just then, Mr. Kipling whipped his tail up, knocking the top scoop off of Jessie's ice cream cone. It landed with a splat on the floor, and he quickly slurped it up.

"Except for him," Jessie announced sternly. "You're grounded, Mr. Kipling. Go to your cage."

Mr. Kipling waddled out of the kitchen with his head down.

"Hey, I'm getting pretty good at this nanny stuff," Jessie said, laughing.

When Jessie arrived in New York, she instantly
made friends with Tony.

Zuri needed a new nanny. "Hey, Jessie,
you want the gig?"

After an intense interview, Jessie got the job! She would be
taking care of four kids: Emma, Luke, Ravi, and Zuri.

Jessie wanted the family to have dinner together.
She had her work cut out for her!

Zuri wished she had a pet pony. After all, her brother
Ravi owned a giant lizard!

"Good luck at the science fair, Emma," said Jessie.
"Remember, Pluto might need a little extra glue."

Emma's presentation was out of this world!

At school, Luke pulled a "Kick Me" sign off Ravi's back.
Ravi explained that he was tired of getting picked on.

Luke talked to Kenny, his stuffed koala. "Daddy
loves you, K-Bear. Be good for Uncle Ravi."

"Eat your math sandwich, Mr. Kipling!" said Zuri as she fed him her homework.

Bullies shot spitballs at Ravi! Zuri was glad that he required Jessie's undivided attention.

Jessie wanted Luke to stand up for Ravi—not to let
Ravi take the heat for him!

Zuri told Rosie, "There are two things I'm good at: eating
cookies and kicking butt. And we're all out of cookies!"

Emma demanded to know why Rosie embarrassed
her at school.

Ravi realized the girls at school liked his sensitive nature.
"I'm proud of you," Luke said.

Dear Diary,

Well, Emma won her science fair; Ravi is my new buddy, Zuri and I have a swim date on Saturday with Millie the Mermaid, and I think Luke is finally done trying to get me to date him. Plus, Christina and Morgan are reducing their travel plans so they can be home more often. Not too bad for my first two days, huh? It may sound crazy, but I think I'm going to like it here—even more than an authentic NYC slice with extra mozzarella!

Jessie

JESSIE

Part 2

Dear Diary,

This week, the kids are going back to school, and I get a much-deserved break from my nanny duties. I see long fall days reading the classics at the New York City Public Library, running in Central Park, seeing all of the exhibits at the Metropolitan Museum of Art, hitting up the matinees for all of the newest Broadway shows, and volunteering at the local soup kitchen in my future. Oh, who am I kidding? These kids have me so worn out, I'll probably spend most of my time napping and reading tabloid magazines . . . I can't wait!

Jessie

Chapter 1

It was the first day of a new school year, and Jessie was running late. She hurried to pack Ravi, Zuri, Emma, and Luke's bags before they had to catch the bus. There were school supplies, lunches, and extra jackets everywhere. Jessie, sighing, scooped most of the mess up from Luke's pile and shoved it all into his bag. She wasn't sure exactly what he needed, but this way he would have anything he might need.

Bertram, the family's formal butler, was humming to himself as he placed omelets in front of each of the Ross kids.

"Bertram, you look so happy. Did your Cheese of the Week come in?" Jessie asked.

"Better," Bertram replied, beaming at her. "It's the day I've waited for since summer began—the end of summer!"

"Try to contain yourself, Bertram," Luke snorted. "You're drooling in our eggs."

"I'm excited too! I have enough back-to-school outfits to last until Easter," Emma added happily.

"My plan for this year is to reduce my wedgie ratio to one per fortnight," Ravi said.

"If you keep using words like 'fortnight,' it's going to be a long, wedgie-rific year," Luke replied.

Zuri wrinkled her nose. "I just don't want a desk next to Gross Gus. He's always shoving stuff up his nose. He claims he doesn't know what happened to my magenta crayon, but I have a theory."

Bertram interrupted her, picking up all of their

plates. "Oh, my, look at the time. Don't want to be tardy on your first day back," he said.

"But I'm still eating," Luke protested. He jumped up and followed Bertram to the sink, snagging the last few bites of his eggs before Bertram scraped the food off the plate and into the trash.

Jessie grabbed Luke's arm and pulled him into the living room with his siblings. She handed out their backpacks and pushed them into the elevator so they could head to school.

"Bye! Love you! Miss you already!" Jessie called as the elevator doors shut. Then she burst into tears.

"I can't believe you're sad to see them go," Bertram said.

"I'm not sad," Jessie sobbed. "These are tears of joy! This has been the longest summer of my life!"

"Jessie, I'm shocked," Bertram said, disbelief written all over his face. "I never thought we'd have something in common! I mean, besides the oversized feet and secret love of boy bands."

"We're finally free!" Jessie said gleefully, wiping away the last of her tears. She grabbed Bertram's hand and they both jumped up and down, squealing happily.

Suddenly, the elevator doors slid open, and the Ross kids caught them celebrating. Jessie and Bertram stopped immediately and hung their heads in shame.

"Told you," Luke said to his siblings.

"That's just cold," Zuri said, shaking her head in disapproval as the elevator doors closed again.

As soon as the doors were shut, Jessie and Bertram began jumping up and down again in excitement. They were free!

Dear Diary,

Ah, the first day of school—new clothes, new classes, and new embarrassments. I just hope the Ross kids' first days aren't as bad as mine were back in Texas. Let's just say that the other kids were not impressed with my hunting couture.

Luckily, Emma, Luke, Ravi, and Zuri all have the most fashionable outfits, and they go to a much more sophisticated school than I did. How bad can it be?

Jessie

Chapter 2

Emma was really excited for a brand-new school year at Walden Academy. A new school year meant new clothes, new sparkly notebooks, and new classes—like art.

She sat down at a two-person art table just as Shelby and her clique walked by. Shelby was one of the most popular girls in Emma's class. She and her friends always wore clothes with their names embroidered on them. Emma didn't have a problem with Shelby, but she did think that her outfits were sometimes a little much.

A tough-looking girl Emma had never seen before followed Shelby's crew into the room. She was dressed all in black with a lot of chains and carried a beat-up tool bag as a purse.

Shelby spotted the new girl and made a disgusted face to her friends. "New-girl alert," she said snidely. "Yikes, that outfit is puke-ular! What's with all the chains? Did you just escape from fashion jail?" Shelby's friends all laughed.

"What's with all the makeup?" the new girl countered. "Did you just escape from clown college?"

Shelby continued to glare at her as the new girl plopped down in the seat next to Emma with a mean-looking scowl on her face.

"I like your chains!" Emma said, trying to be friendly. "Totally worth the half-hour backup at the metal detector, I'm sure." The new girl's look wasn't really Emma's thing either, but she had to admit it was stylish in a grunge sort of way. "I'm Emma."

"Rosie," the new girl said by way of introduction, her voice dripping with sarcasm. "I wear chains as a symbol of oppressed people everywhere. Plus, my diamond tiara is out for cleaning."

"I hate it when they don't give you a loaner," Emma said sincerely.

Rosie looked at her in complete disbelief, but before she could say anything in response, the art teacher, Ms. Devlin, walked in. Ms. Devlin had a reputation for being a little bitter about her own failed art career.

"I'm Ms. Devlin; welcome to high school art, everyone," she announced. "I look at all your enthusiastic faces and I think to myself, I hate my life. If only my art career had taken off. That said, let's have some fun! You have thirty seconds to draw a picture that tells me who you really are. Show me your essence!"

"So, where are you from?" Emma asked Rosie as they started drawing.

"Well, you go to Fifth Avenue, and keep walking north until you realize your purse is missing," Rosie responded without looking up.

"Luckily, if you're on Fifth Avenue, you can just buy another one," Emma said matter-of-factly.

"Sounds like more talking than soul-searching going on over here," Ms. Devlin said as she walked over to Emma and Rosie's table. "If I cared enough, you'd both be in trouble. Rosie, let's see your work."

"It's a skull and crossbones over a dollar sign,"

Rosie said, holding up her picture. "It represents my wish for the death of capitalism and corporate greed."

"Bummer. Emma, what does your essence look like?"

"A smiley daisy," Emma answered.

"Wow," Rosie said sarcastically. "You are about as deep as a kiddie pool."

"Stop," Emma protested. "You're making my daisy sad."

"Okay, class, working with your desk partner, your first big project will be to create an artistic statement about something you feel is wrong with the world," Ms. Devlin said, assigning them their first homework.

"So, Rosie, you want to work at my place?" Emma said brightly. "I'd go to yours, but I kinda like this purse."

"What I want is a different partner," Rosie said to Ms. Devlin, ignoring Emma altogether.

"And I want my still-life portraits hanging at the Louvre. Deal with it," Ms. Devlin replied.

Emma glared at Rosie. Why was the new girl being so mean?

♥ ♥ ♥

Luke and Ravi's first day wasn't going much better. When they met up at their lockers between classes, Luke had to pull a "Kick Me" sign off of Ravi's back.

"Dude, already?" Luke asked.

"Oh, I put that there," Ravi answered matter-of-factly. "My scalp and I are tired of noogies, so I thought I would give the football team a new option."

Luke shook his head and pulled his jacket out of his backpack. As he did, his favorite stuffed bear, Kenny the Koala, fell out of his bag, tangled up in his gym shorts and socks.

"Kenny the Koala?" Ravi asked, picking the bear up and handing him to Luke. "First-day jitters, brother?"

"No!" Luke exclaimed, trying to untangle Kenny. "Jessie must have accidentally shoved him in with all my stuff."

Ravi laughed. "Whatever you have to tell yourself, bro."

One of Luke and Ravi's classmates, Billy, walked by with some of his friends and spotted Luke holding Kenny.

"Hey, Little Lukey, did you bring your teddy bear to school today?" Billy asked mockingly.

Luke pulled Kenny to his chest, embarrassed. "What bear? Oh, Kenny? I mean, this random bear? Never saw him before in my life," Luke said loudly. Then he looked down at Kenny and whispered, "I'm sorry; just go with it."

"Really. Then whose teddy-weddy is he?" Billy asked. Billy's friends laughed.

Ravi looked at his brother and realized how embarrassed Luke was. Ravi grabbed Kenny away from Luke.

"Kenny is my teddy-weddy," Ravi said. "Or to be more precise, my koala-walla."

The bell rang, and Billy and his friends laughed as they headed off to class.

"We got ourselves a bear-lover, boys!" Billy shouted over his shoulder. "It's gonna be a good year!"

Luke collapsed back against his locker in relief. "Thanks, Ravi! Wow, I can't believe you took that hit for me!"

"Well, you are my brother and you have your

reputation to uphold as a Big Man on Campus," Ravi replied. "Whereas I am Barely a Man on Campus."

"Well, good talk. I gotta get to class," Luke said, getting his swagger back. "Let's hug it out. Bring it in, bro."

Ravi stretched out his arms for a hug. Luke reached out and grabbed Kenny, cuddling the stuffed bear close.

"I was talking to Kenny," Luke said. "Daddy loves you, K-Bear. Be good for Uncle Ravi."

Dear Diary,

My first day off was pure bliss. There was no one there to steal the remote when I was watching my favorite show, no one to eat my snack when I got up to go to the bathroom . . . and no one to talk to besides Bertram. I will admit that I missed the kids a little. I may have gotten a teensy bit bored without them around, but I'm sure they'll make up for it when they get home. I've already gotten an e-mail from Zuri's teacher with her homework assignments. Somehow I can't imagine Zuri is too happy about that, and I'm sure I'll hear all about it when she gets home!

Jessie

Chapter 3

Jessie was really enjoying her time off, even if the house was a little too quiet without the kids around. She'd plopped herself down in a big squishy chair in the Ross's screening room and had been watching infomercials on their giant TV all afternoon. There were so many good deals on the infomercial channel. Jessie had already ordered a battery-powered foot-massager, a sweater folding board, and a crystal-encrusted cell phone case. She was in the process of ordering a really cool cutting machine for root vegetables.

"It slices *and* dices?" Jessie was saying to the infomercial operator over the phone as Zuri walked in. "I can't afford not to! Wait, how much is shipping and handling? That's ridiculous—I live in New York, not Siberia!"

Jessie hung up the phone. No matter how cool the cutting tool was, she couldn't afford thirty-five dollars for shipping.

"Zuri! Welcome home," she said brightly. "How was your first day of school?"

"Horrible! I got homework! That I can't do with crayons!" Zuri whined. "It's downright un-American. Our Founding Fathers built this great country on the separation of home and work."

"No, they didn't," Jessie replied calmly. "And obviously, we should start with history."

"I'm not interested in anything that happened B.Z. You know, Before Zuri," Zuri said. "Who cares about a bunch of old guys in wigs?"

"Those 'old guys' had to combine thirteen colonies into a country. You just have to combine five vocab words into a sentence. Any more arguments?" Jessie asked.

"Give me liberty or give me death!" Zuri exclaimed. She grabbed the remote and changed the channel to cartoons.

"Give me a break. And the remote," Jessie demanded. She plucked the remote from Zuri's hand and replaced it with Zuri's homework. Zuri stuck her tongue out as Jessie walked toward the living room to greet the other kids. "But keep that tongue in your mouth," Jessie added without turning around.

Jessie walked into the living room to find Emma and Rosie coming out of the elevator.

"Whoa," Rosie said, looking around the

penthouse in amazement. "This room is bigger than my whole apartment. And I live with my mom, dad, grandma, three brothers, two sisters, and four rats—six if it's really cold."

"We don't have any rats, but we have a Bertram," Jessie replied with a laugh. "He has beady eyes and whiskers and he loves cheese."

"Rosie's here to work on a project," Emma explained. "Rosie, this is Jessie, my nanny."

"A nanny?" Rosie asked. "Where do you keep the footmen and the stable boys?"

"Emma, you haven't told her about the country estate?" Jessie said, teasing them.

"Hey, Rosie," Emma said. "Before we start, why don't we sit at the table and have a little chitchat?" She was determined to find a way to get along with her grumpy partner.

Rosie hesitated but sat down at the table with

Emma. They looked at each other silently for an awkward moment.

"So . . ." Emma finally asked. "What do you like to do for fun?"

"Stick it to the man," Rosie answered.

"Oh-kay," Emma replied slowly. She was going to keep asking questions until she found some common ground with Rosie. "But do you ever, like, play volleyball? Or go to the movies? Or, you know . . . not make people uncomfortable?"

"No, but I am setting up a rally in Times Square to protest deforestation," Rosie said.

"Speaking of deforestation, have you ever thought of plucking your eyebrows?" Emma said brightly, thinking they may have something to talk about after all.

But Rosie looked offended. "No, I'm very happy with the one I have."

"But my mom says everyone loves a makeover," Emma protested. The conversation was not going at all the way she wanted it to. "That's how she sold enough beauty products to pay for the new helipad."

"Hashtag Most Obnoxious Sentence Ever," Rosie said, rolling her eyes.

"Hashtag Nuh-uh!" Emma shot back.

"Look, princess, you and I will never have anything in common," Rosie said, checking her watch and standing up. "Let's talk tomorrow, okay? To get back to the Bronx, I have to take three trains to where my aunt picks me up on her scooter."

"So the Bronx is a real place?" Emma asked, her eyes wide in disbelief. "I thought it was imaginary, like Narnia or Staten Island."

The next day, Emma was not looking forward to art class. She arrived early, ready to get a fresh start with Rosie, but as soon as Rosie walked in, Emma realized the odds weren't in her favor.

"Oh, you all showed up. In that case, take your seats," Ms. Devlin said in a bored voice. "You should keep working on your projects. Maybe someday you'll be as successful as Bobo the Chimp. His finger paintings edged out my landscapes for a spot at the Guggenheim. I really hate that monkey."

"I think Ms. Devlin could use some bran," Emma whispered to Rosie as she sat down next to her. "She looks constipated."

Rosie pulled her phone out of her bag and turned on the record feature. "Hey, do you mind if I record our brainstorming sessions?" Rosie asked Emma. "I don't want to miss any of your supersmart ideas."

"Sure!" Emma said brightly. Maybe she and Rosie would end up as friends after all. "Jessie's always saying she can't believe the stuff that comes out of my mouth."

"I'll bet. You know, I have an awesome idea for our presentation," Rosie said, leaning forward conspiratorially. "But to make it work, you'd have to dress up like a beautiful doll."

"I can do that! I love fashion!" Emma said, clapping with excitement. "Um, but is it all right if I pick out my own outfit?"

"Whatever you think is best," Rosie nodded. "You're the fashion guru. And since you're going to be the presenter, I will take care of everything else."

"Really? That's so nice! I knew we would find a way to work together. Everyone should really stop calling you a heinous she-devil," Emma said. She glanced up and saw an annoyed look on Rosie's face. "Aw, do you need some bran, too?" Emma asked sweetly.

Dear Diary,

Things are looking up for Emma. She and Rosie are getting along, and they have their art project all figured out. That's one problem I can stop worrying about. Zuri's homework issue, on the other hand, is only getting worse. She didn't turn in any homework today, and her teacher e-mailed me saying Zuri's grades will suffer if she doesn't bring her homework in as soon as possible. Still, at least one problem is better than two. And the boys haven't had any that I know of—so maybe I can get back to worry-free days sooner than I thought!

Jessie

Chapter 4

Bertram was in the kitchen putting away groceries when Zuri arrived home from her second day of school. She walked into the kitchen a few minutes later, leading Mr. Kipling on a leash and holding her worksheets from her classes.

"Bertram, can I have the peanut butter?" Zuri asked sweetly.

"Okay, but don't spoil your dinner," Bertram replied, handing her a jar of crunchy peanut butter.

Zuri sniffed the air and scrunched up her nose.

"Smells like your liver soufflé did that already."

"I always enjoy our little chats," Bertram said sarcastically. He shook his head and walked out of the room.

As soon as Bertram was gone, Zuri opened the peanut butter and smeared it all over her worksheets. Then she set them down in front of Mr. Kipling. He whipped out his tongue and pulled the first sheet into his mouth, crunching loudly as he ate the paper.

"Eat your math sandwich, Mr. Kipling!" Zuri cooed at him. She held up her vocabulary sheet. "And if you clean your plate, you can have some vocab sheets for dessert. I'm sure they will be 'traumatic' and 'loquacious.' Yum!"

Just then, Jessie walked in and stopped short when she saw what Zuri was doing.

"What's Mr. Kipling eating?" Jessie demanded.

Zuri looked up and put her hands to her cheeks, pretending to be horrified. "Oh, no!" Zuri exclaimed. "The lizard ate my homework!"

"Well, that'll be one the teacher hasn't heard," Jessie said. "Luckily, she e-mailed me your worksheets, but nice try."

"Stupid Internet!" Zuri fumed. "I wish I was born in olden times, like you and Bertram!"

"What do I have to do to get you to do your homework? It's not that much!" Jessie begged.

"Wrong. The teacher assigned us more today, so now it's twice as much work," Zuri said.

"At least we know you can do math," Jessie muttered.

Luke and Ravi walked into the kitchen behind her. Ravi was covered head-to-toe in spitballs. He looked miserable.

"School stinks!" Zuri shouted. "Just ask Ravi!"

Jessie spun around, her eyes going wide in surprise as she saw Ravi. "Ravi, what happened to you?" Jessie put an arm around him and guided him toward the table.

"A spitball ambush," Ravi replied.

Jessie immediately pulled her arm back and wiped it off.

"Well, looks like this needs your full, undivided attention," Zuri said to Jessie. Then she turned to Ravi as she skipped off to watch TV. "Thank you for being you."

Jessie sighed as she watched Zuri leave. "One thing at a time. Okay, who did this to you, Ravi?"

"The important thing is, it is not the fault of Luke," Ravi said as he pulled spitballs from his shirt.

"Luke, what did you do?" Jessie demanded.

"It wasn't me!" Luke protested. "Some kids at

school have been giving Ravi a hard time because I may have sorta, kinda been seen with Kenny at school and then sorta, kinda let Ravi take the heat for it."

"Luke!" Jessie exclaimed. "That is sorta, kinda despicable!"

"Well, it's your fault!" he countered.

"How is that even remotely possible?!" Jessie asked defensively.

"You're the one who put Kenny in my bag!" Luke replied.

"Okay . . ." Jessie said slowly, realizing that it actually *was* her fault. "That's not so remote. But how could you just stand by and let Ravi get wallpapered?"

"Excuse me, but in defense of Luke—" Ravi said.

"Not now. I've got to get to the bottom of

this," Jessie interrupted. "Luke, you need to stand up for your brother."

"I didn't ask him to do this. He volunteered. He's fine with it," Luke protested.

"If I may interject—" Ravi spoke up.

"Clearly, he's not fine," Jessie said, interrupting Ravi again. "He's covered in saliva and shame!"

"Is anyone concerned that if I do not shower soon I may harden into a giant papier-mâché garden gnome?" Ravi loudly moaned. Jessie and Luke just looked at him blankly. "So, just me?"

"Luke, I'm disappointed in you. I always thought the best part of having siblings must be having someone to stick up for you. Ravi did his part; now it's your turn," Jessie said sternly.

"But I can't! You just don't get it!" Luke shouted and ran up to his room.

Jessie sighed.

"Jessie, since you were an only child, who stuck up for you in school?" Ravi asked.

"My dad. He'd show up on campus, lob an old avocado at the cheerleaders, and yell 'Fire in the hole!'" Jessie said, laughing diabolically at the memory. "You've never seen a pyramid topple so fast."

"Sometimes you scare me," Ravi said.

Jessie walked out of the room, still laughing. Ravi shook his head and then tried to stand up, but he couldn't. The spitballs had dried and left him stuck to his seat.

"Guys!" Ravi yelled, pulling at his pants. "Oh, no! I'm stuck. Guys?!"

"And you thought your life would get easier once the kids were back in school," Bertram said to Jessie as they shared a snack in the kitchen later that night.

Jessie rubbed her temples. She had a splitting headache, and she was exhausted. "I was wrong. Bigger problems, bigger bags under my eyes, but oddly enough, same salary," she said ruefully.

Zuri tiptoed into the kitchen and headed for the pantry.

"Hold up, missy," Jessie said. She pointed at a chair, and Zuri walked over and sat down. "Please, please, *please* tell me your homework's done," Jessie begged.

"Do you want the truth? Or do you just want to feel better?" Zuri asked.

Jessie slammed her head down on the table dramatically. Zuri patted her on the back. "Aw, Jessie, I hate to see you like this," Zuri said. "I'll have my snack on the terrace." Then she swept out of the room, carrying Jessie's bedtime snack with her.

Dear Diary,

So much for my earlier optimism—Zuri still hasn't done any homework, and it turns out that Ravi is being bullied and it's all Luke's fault . . . okay, maybe it's a little bit my fault, too. I just can't believe Luke let his brother take the fall for him. If he doesn't do the right thing soon, I may need to take a page out of my dad's book and show up at school. I guess I should start saving avocados—you know, just in case. . . .

Jessie

Chapter 5

uke had never been so ashamed of himself. He felt really badly that everyone was picking on Ravi, but he knew that if he said anything, they'd pick on him instead. And he would feel even worse about that. He leaned his head against his locker and sighed.

"Hey, wittle Wavi!" Billy said loudly. "Wanna play some dodge-bear?"

Billy had cornered Ravi midway down the hall, and Ravi was cringing in fear. Billy pulled a small stuffed bear from his bag and chucked it at Ravi's head. Then all of Billy's friends did the same. There were bears flying everywhere. Ravi cowered, holding his arms up to protect his face.

"Only nine more months of this. Perhaps the librarian will let me eat lunch with her again this year," Ravi muttered.

Luke watched in horror. He couldn't let them tease Ravi like that anymore. He had to do something! He reached into his locker, grabbed Kenny, and climbed up on top of a nearby chair. He whistled loudly.

"Hey! Everyone! Listen up!" Luke yelled. He lifted Kenny up into the air. "Kenny is mine. He doesn't belong to Ravi."

The crowd gasped.

"Luke, you do not have to do this," Ravi urged him.

Luke bent forward. "Yes, I do." Then he stood

back up and addressed the crowd. "Kenny's been with me since I was a baby. He hangs out on my bed, and sometimes I bring him to the dentist when I'm nervous because I haven't flossed."

Some of the girls who were listening giggled and began whispering to one another.

"In fact, the only person who's been a better friend to me than Kenny is Ravi. So quit making fun of my brother!"

The crowd was silent for a moment, and then the group of girls let out a loud "Awwwwww!"

"They think this is *cute*?" Billy said in disbelief.

Luke hopped down off of his chair and walked over to the waiting girls. He took one on each arm and let another hug Kenny on his way to class.

"Classic Luke," Ravi said, shaking his head and following Luke down the hall. "With those freckles and that charisma, he makes it work."

Emma was ready for her big art presentation. She'd stayed up late designing the perfect doll costume. She just hoped Rosie liked it as much as she did. She had on a blond beauty-queen wig teased high and was wearing a pink tutu, a tank top, a jacket, and hot-pink pumps.

Rosie was standing at their desk in front of a six-foot-high, three-sided pink box. The front was covered in a thick sheet of clear plastic.

"Rosie, does this look okay?" Emma asked, smoothing down her skirt.

"Perfect," Rosie said appreciatively.

"Now can you please tell me what we're doing?" Emma asked.

"Emma, I am the artist, you are the art," Rosie explained patiently. "This will work best if you just keep your mind completely blank."

"Sorry, what was that?" Emma asked. She had gotten distracted by Shelby's embroidered headband. "I was thinking about headbands."

"See? You're a natural," Rosie said. "Okay, showtime. Hop in the box."

Emma shrugged, stepped into the box, and posed with a big smile. Rosie grabbed a roll of pink duct tape and taped the plastic to the side of the box, sealing Emma inside. Then Rosie revealed a sign on the front that read "Ditsy Doll." Emma couldn't see it.

Rosie pulled a string on the side of the box, and Emma's voice came from a small speaker on the side. Her voice sounded odd and stilted, obviously having been edited together from Rosie's recordings.

"Women are objects, not people," the recording said.

"What was that?" Emma asked from inside the box. She could barely hear anything.

"It's just part of the project," Rosie said loudly. "Just move your mouth up and down when I pull the cord."

"Like this?" Emma asked, opening and closing her mouth several times. As they finished setting up, Emma posed prettily, and the rest of the class and Ms. Devlin gathered around.

Rosie pulled the cord again, and Emma moved her mouth as directed.

"Who needs brains when you're pretty?" the recording asked.

Everyone laughed.

"That is so true, Emma," Shelby said, nodding sincerely.

Rosie pulled the cord again, but Emma wasn't playing along anymore. She stepped forward and put her ear against the wall of the box, trying to hear what the recording said.

"What do we have here?" Ms. Devlin asked.

"We object to the fact that women are judged by the way they look rather than what's in their heads," Rosie explained, gesturing to Emma.

Their teacher raised her eyebrows and nodded. "Too true. I, for one, was judged harshly in the art world during an unfortunate sweatpants phase. Apparently, Picasso can have a Blue Period, but I can't have an Elastic Waistband Period!" Ms. Devlin grumbled.

Rosie pulled the string again.

"It's better to be beautiful than nice," the recording said.

"Hey!" Emma shouted through the plastic. "That's my voice, but I never said that!" She pushed at the plastic, trying to escape the box.

"Emma looks a bit upset," Ms. Devlin said to Rosie pointedly.

"I want out!" Emma yelled.

"'Out' of this role she's been forced to play," Rosie scrambled to cover to their teacher. "But the, uh, duct tape of society won't let her!"

Emma stepped back and ran at the side of the box. She slammed through the plastic, knocking her wig off and nearly falling on her face. The entire class laughed as she struggled to stand back up on her heels. She turned bright red with embarrassment and ran out of the room.

"Rosie," Ms. Devlin said sternly. "Since you're a Ross Foundation Scholarship student—you know that the Rosses are her parents—so you should probably go after her."

Rosie hung her head and walked out, following Emma.

Dear Diary,

Looks like I won't need those avocados after all. Ravi called and told me that Luke stood up for him, admitted Kenny was his, and somehow ended up with more dates than the most popular guy in his school. Luke definitely takes after his dad—he is one smooth kid. I know that was tough, but I think it brought Ravi and Luke closer together as brothers. It was a good reminder for me, too—sometimes you have to face problems head-on to get to the best stuff in life. That's what I'm going to do with Zuri—face the homework problem head-on.

Jessie

Chapter 6

Jessie had a plan. She was not letting Zuri go another day without completing her homework. She had no choice—if Zuri failed out of school, Jessie was pretty sure the Rosses would fire her. So she waited patiently by the elevator to snag Zuri as soon as she stepped off of it.

Finally, with a loud ding, the elevator doors opened. Zuri was standing inside, but as soon as she saw Jessie waiting, she lunged for the buttons, frantically pushing the "door close" button.

"Close, close, close, close, close!" Zuri

muttered, but Jessie was too quick for her. Jessie stepped forward, picked Zuri up, and carried her, struggling, to her desk.

"Help, help! Nanny gone berserk!" Zuri wailed.

"Here's the deal: neither one of us moves until you finish your homework," Jessie said, plopping Zuri down in the desk chair.

"Works for me, but don't you have tickets to see that new musical next month?" Zuri said tartly.

"One second," Jessie said. She turned and walked calmly to the sofa, where she picked up a pillow. Then she turned and screamed into the pillow, jumping up and down in rage and frustration. That kid knew how to push all of her buttons. Then Jessie dropped the pillow and walked back to the desk. "Homework. Now."

"Jessie, please don't make me," Zuri begged.

"Sweetie, I'm getting a feeling this is about more than just not wanting to do your homework. Why don't you tell me what's really bothering you?" Jessie asked, squatting down in front of Zuri.

"Well . . . third grade is a lot tougher than second," Zuri said, fidgeting nervously. "What if I'm not smart enough to do the work?"

"Zuri, you're the smartest little girl I know. Look, we'll do it together, and every time you get a question right, you'll get five extra minutes of TV time. How does that sound?" Jessie replied.

"I usually prefer my bribes in cash, but I can get behind TV time. *Hillbilly Idol* is on tonight," Zuri said agreeably.

Ten minutes later, Zuri put down her pencil, smiling. "Done! That was so easy! Why did you make such a big deal out of it?"

Jessie's mouth dropped open in disbelief. Zuri handed her a pillow. "Do you feel another scream coming on?"

Just then, the elevator opened and Emma stomped out, her costume askew and her face still flushed in embarrassment. She looked like a very angry Barbie doll.

"Emma, what's the matter?" Jessie asked, rushing over to her. "You look like Ken died."

"Rosie humiliated me in front of the entire school!" Emma explained.

"Oh sweetie, I'm so sorry," Jessie said, pulling Emma into a hug. "I remember one time, my best friend Darla embarrassed me at school. It was laundry day, and I was wearing my granny underpants—"

The ding of the elevator interrupted her.

"Saved by the bell!" Zuri exclaimed. None

of the Ross kids wanted to hear another one of Jessie's stories about life in Texas.

The elevator doors slid open, and Rosie walked into the penthouse looking sheepish.

"Emma—" Rosie said tentatively.

"I don't want to talk to you!" Emma interrupted.

"Emma, is this the girl who was mean to you?" Zuri asked. Emma nodded, and Zuri turned to face Rosie. "Listen, you. There are two things I'm good at: eating cookies and kicking butt. And we're all out of cookies!"

Zuri jumped at Rosie, but Jessie caught her midair and walked with her toward the screening room. "Okay, Tenacious Z and I will be watching TV in the screening room," Jessie said. "Not eavesdropping . . . much."

"This is not over!" Zuri shouted.

"I like her," Rosie said. "She's got spunk."

Emma glared at her, her arms crossed. "Fine. What do you need to say to me?"

"Well, first of all, we got an A, and second, I want to apologize. I didn't mean to hurt your feelings," Rosie said.

"Well, you did!" Emma snapped. "I am so taking back my friend request!"

"I was going to accept, really," Rosie pleaded. "But my grandma won't get off our computer! She keeps looking for a boyfriend on that dating site, I've-Fallen-in-Love-and-I-Can't-Get-Up."

"Why would you embarrass me like that?" Emma asked.

"I was trying to make a statement about people like you and Shelby," Rosie said and sighed.

"I'm nothing like Shelby," Emma said, her voice thick with anger. "My shirts say 'Emma.' And, unlike Shelby, I tried to be nice to you."

Rosie looked down. "I know. I guess I just never thought someone like me could hurt someone like you. Your life is so . . . perfect."

Emma snorted. "My life isn't perfect. My nanny was just giving me a speech about her underpants."

"Yeah, she's weird," Rosie agreed. "Okay, the truth is, I'm jealous, all right? You live here, and you look like that, and you're so nice, I just want to . . . smack you all the time!" Rosie gestured around the penthouse and at Emma as she spoke. Emma could tell she was being sincere.

"Please don't smack me. If you really want to smack someone, may I suggest Shelby?" Emma said, beginning to thaw a little. "I mean, she's totally puke-ular."

"Do you know what's puke-ular? The word 'puke-ular'," Rosie said, giggling.

"I know, right?" Emma agreed. "And you know what? I think your fashion statements are cool."

"Thanks!" Rosie said, blushing a little. "Do you maybe wanna borrow the skirt I made out of compost?"

"Uhhh . . ." Emma said, trying to figure out a nice way to say no. She was so *not* wearing a compost skirt. "That seems like it's more for . . . spring." She paused and then smiled. "Huh. We both love fashion and detest Shelby. Turns out, we have lots in common."

Jessie stuck her head through the curtained doorway that separated the living room and screening room. "Told you so!" she said gleefully. Clearly, she and Zuri had been eavesdropping.

"Do you mind? I'm trying to talk to my friend!" Emma asked, rolling her eyes. Then she turned to Rosie and whispered, "Don't you hate it when your nanny and butler eavesdrop on you?"

"Okay, if we're going to be friends, please cool it with the rich-people problems. It's super-annoying," Rosie said.

"I used to feel the same way," Jessie interjected. "Try the massage chairs in the screening room. You'll get over it."

❤ ❤ ❤

Ravi had never felt so popular. He stood at his locker snuggling a cute teddy bear and surrounded by girls.

". . . And sometimes," he was saying to the girls, "when I watch a movie where a doggy and kitty make friends, I cry a little. Please do not think less of me."

"Awww!" the girls cooed. Ravi smiled proudly and took a few steps over to meet Luke.

"Nice work, bro," Luke complimented Ravi,

putting a hand on Ravi's shoulder. "I'm proud of you."

"Yes, vulnerability is catnip to the ladies," Ravi said eagerly. "Next week, I will feign a sports injury."

The bell chimed and a scratchy voice came on the school's speaker. "Attention. Ravi Ross, please report to the office. Your nanny has dropped off your odor-control shoe inserts and wants to remind you that you're a special little boy, and don't let anyone tell you any different."

The girls Ravi had been talking to gave him a disgusted look and wandered away, giggling. Ravi turned bright red and leaned his head against his locker.

"Hope you enjoyed it while it lasted," Luke said, cringing in sympathy.

"The gods giveth, and Jessie taketh away," Ravi said, shaking his head.

Dear Diary,

Well, the kids survived their first week at school, and it wasn't too traumatic. I've got Zuri on a strict homework schedule, and she's doing great. Emma has found a new friend in Rosie, and she's even agreed to plan a protest with her. Plus, Ravi and Luke made a pact to always stick up for each other. And Luke doesn't have to leave Kenny the Koala at home anymore—Kenny may be the first stuffed koala to ever graduate from Walden Academy. Needless to say, with all of the problems solved, the Home Shopping Channel is calling my name.

Jessie

The story continues!

Look for the next book in Disney's *Jessie* series!

Crush
Crazy

Adapted by Lexi Ryals

Based on the series created by Pamela Eells O'Connell

Part One is based on the episode "Creepy Connie Comes a Callin'," written by Eric Scharr & David J. Booth

Part Two is based on the episode "The Trouble with Tessie," written by David J. Booth & Eric Schaar

Dear Diary,

Things are going so well with my job I think I should get an award, or something. Emma is busy with lots of extracurricular activities. Zuri finally stopped fighting me on her schoolwork and is getting good grades. Ravi is performing excellently at school, as usual. Luke has gotten really into break dancing and wants to practice all of the time. The only problem is that Luke's grades have started to slip—I really need to find him a tutor, especially in math. But hey, one problem instead of a hundred is serious improvement. I think I'll go see if I can find some nanny competitions online—I would easily win!

Jessie

Chapter 1

Jessie was sitting on a sunny bench in Central Park, enjoying the last of the autumn sun as she watched Luke break dancing with two of his friends. She had to admit it—the kid had some serious moves. There were several clusters of middle school girls watching and letting out squeals as Luke executed a series of flips, ending with splits.

"Careful!" Jessie called. "If you break your neck, your parents will break mine!"

A cute girl named Connie with long blond

hair plopped down next to Jessie. She had her smartphone out and was recording the dancing.

"Doesn't Luke have the most amazing moves?" the girl asked her dreamily.

"Yeah, you should see how he wiggles out of doing chores," Jessie, said laughing.

The girl pulled a flip-cam out of her bag and held it up with her other hand, filming Luke with both cameras.

"So why two cameras?" Jessie asked.

"I can't decide which is his best side," Connie explained matter-of-factly. "Plus, if I blink and miss something, I have two backups."

"Good thinking. Here I am, blinking and missing everything," Jessie said sarcastically, but the girl beamed at her, totally oblivious. "So . . . are you a friend of Luke's?"

"I wish!" the girl exclaimed. "I'm Connie. We're in the same math class."

"I'm Jessie, his nanny, and considering his grades, I'm stunned he even goes to math class."

"Oh, he does! I've got the video to prove it," Connie said fondly. "I've got Luke texting, throwing spitballs, going sleepy-bye . . ."

"I didn't know he could go sleepy-bye without Kenny the Koala," Jessie mused. When she saw the odd look Connie was giving her, she hurried to cover. "Which is certainly not a stuffed bear he still sleeps with, because that would be an inappropriate thing to reveal. The point is, he should be paying attention in class!"

"You know," Connie said sweetly, "I'm an A-plus student. I could help Luke get his grades up. And do his chores."

"I love you!" Jessie exclaimed, hugging Connie.

"Could you come over tomorrow and help Luke study?"

"Let me check my schedule . . ." Connie replied, trying to play it cool. "Yes!"

Luke finished his solo dance to wild applause.

"Hey Luke," Jessie yelled over to him. "I got you a study buddy!"

Luke smiled broadly until he saw that Jessie was pointing at Connie, and then his look of delight turned to horror.

"Creepy Connie?" Luke asked as he lost his balance and fell over mid-dance move.

"He knows my name!" Connie exclaimed, obviously thrilled.